Let's Make a Friend!

By Erin Guendelsberger
Illustrated by Joe Mathieu

Let's Make a
Friend!

Hello, I'm Guy Smiley,
and welcome to **Let's Make a Friend**,
the show that asks contestants how
they would make a friend!

Our celebrity judges will decide if they
would be the contestant's friend.

Make at least two friends, and
you win the grand prize!

Let's meet today's
contestant. Please welcome...
Elmo from Sesame Street!

Hello, Mr. Smiley!
Elmo is very happy
to be here.

ELMO

Wonderful!
Happy to have you, Elmo.
Now, let's meet the judges.

First, taking a brief vacation
from his trash can, it's…
Oscar the Grouch!

Next, an aspiring fairy,
here is…Abby Cadabby!

ELMo

And, last but not
least, on the trail of a crumb-filled
adventure, please welcome…
Cookie Monster!

It's time to start playing **Let's Make a Friend**!

Elmo, what is the first thing you would do if you wanted to make a new friend?

If Elmo wanted to make a new friend, Elmo would smile and say, "hello."

ELMo

A smile and a hello. Okay. This first response goes to Oscar the Grouch. Oscar, what do you think?

Smiling and saying hello?
That's a terrible idea!

I would rather hear
someone say, "*SCRAM!*"

My answer is **NO**,
I would NOT be
Elmo's friend!

Well, okay, Oscar.
Elmo, I'm sorry, but
that is one **NO**.

ELMO

On to the next question! Elmo, how would you make friends with someone who is feeling shy?

When Elmo feels shy, Elmo likes it if someone asks what kinds of things Elmo likes to do.

ELMo

Elmo says that when someone is shy, you can ask them what kinds of things they like to do. What do you think, Abby?

OSCAR THE GROUCH!

Abby Cadabby!

I remember when I moved to Sesame Street. I was feeling very shy.

It would be magical if someone asked me what I like to do.

Yes, I would be Elmo's friend.

Congratulations, Elmo! That is your first **YES**! You now have *one* friend! Make another friend to win the grand prize!

ELMo

Elmo, are you ready for your third question?

Yes, Mr. Smiley.

ELMO

Elmo, what is something
you could do for a friend
who is feeling sad?

Elmo doesn't like it when a friend feels sad. If Elmo's friend were sad, Elmo would give that friend a hug.

Elmo chooses giving a hug.
This response goes to Cookie Monster.
Cookie Monster, what do you think?

OSCAR THE GROUCH!

Abby Cadabby!

Me would prefer a cookie. Do you have a cookie?

Now, now, Cookie Monster. Let's calm down. There are no cookies for the judges. The only cookies we have are backstage for…

And there he goes!
Cookie Monster has left
the stage!

COOKIES!

Don't worry, Elmo. We have a backup judge! Everyone, please welcome...Big Bird!

ELMo

Hi, everyone. It's so nice to be here. I love to play games.

WELCOME

OSCAR THE GROUCH!

Abby Cadabby!

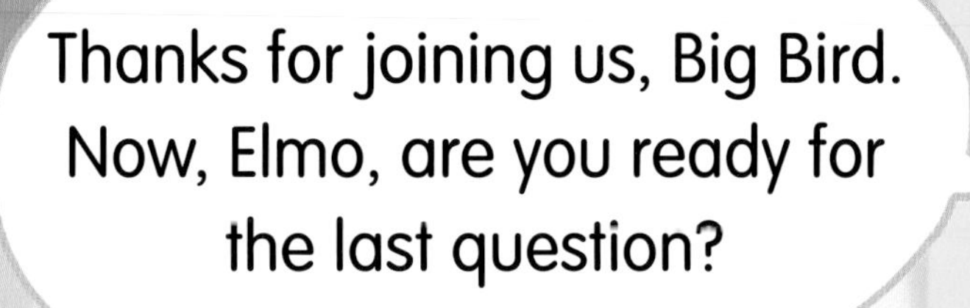
Thanks for joining us, Big Bird. Now, Elmo, are you ready for the last question?
I think so.
ELMo

Elmo, what is the
most important thing about
being a friend?

That's a tough one, Mr. Smiley.

Elmo knows it's important to be kind.

It's also important to share and to listen.

Elmo thinks there isn't one thing but LOTS of things that are important to being a friend.

ELMO

A bold answer, Elmo.
Big Bird, based on that answer,
would you be Elmo's friend?

Wow, Elmo. That's a really good answer.

I always try to be kind to my friends, and I really like it when my friends share with me.

I would like to be Elmo's friend!

That's *two* friends, folks! Elmo has just won **Let's Make a Friend!**

Congratulations, Elmo! We're happy to share today's grand prize—a beautiful basket filled with delicious, homemade chocolate chip cookies!

Bring out Elmo's prize!

Thank you! Thank you very much! That's our show! We'll see you next time, when we find out how Grouches make friends!

ELMo
What?!
OSCAR THE GROUCH!
Abby Cadabby!

Text by Erin Guendelsberger
Illustrations by Joe Mathieu

Published by Sourcebooks Jabberwocky, an imprint of Sourcebooks, Inc.
P.O. Box 4410, Naperville, Illinois 60567-4410
(630) 961-3900
Fax: (630) 961-2168
www.jabberwockykids.com

Source of Production: Worzalla, Stevens Point, WI
Date of Production: May 2016
Run Number: 5006669

Printed and bound in the United States of America.
WOZ 10 9 8 7 6 5 4 3 2 1

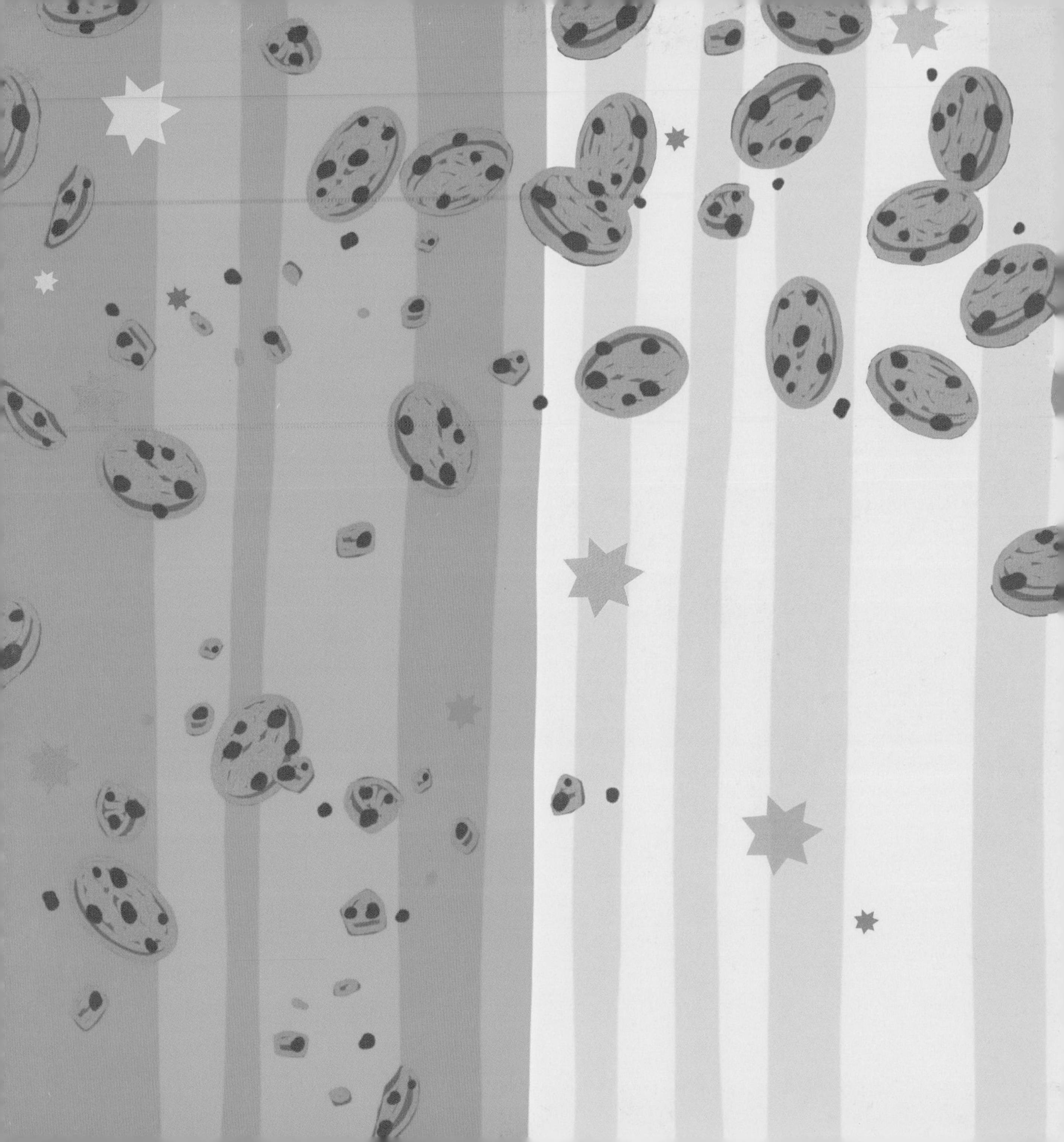